Fitz Roy Carrington

The Kings' Lyrics

Lyrical Poems of the Reigns of King James I and King Charles I

Fitz Roy Carrington

The Kings' Lyrics
Lyrical Poems of the Reigns of King James I and King Charles I

ISBN/EAN: 9783744783125

Printed in Europe, USA, Canada, Australia, Japan

Cover: Foto ©Andreas Hilbeck / pixelio.de

More available books at **www.hansebooks.com**

THE
KINGS'
Lyrics

Lyrical Poems of the Reigns of
KING JAMES I. *and*
KING CHARLES I.
**Together with the Ballad of Agincourt writ-
ten by Michael Drayton. Selected & arranged**
by FitzRoy Carrington

The presse hath gathered into one, what fancie had scat-
tered into many loose papers. — *William Habington.*

Printed for R. H. RUSSELL
NEW YORK
1899

The Preface

J'ay seulement faict icy un amas de fleurs, n'y ayant
fourny du mien que le filet à les lier.

MICHEL DE MONTAIGNE.

I T is singular," writes Mr. Swin-
burne, "that the first great age
of English lyric poetry should have
been also the one great age of
English dramatic poetry: but it is
hardly less singular that the lyric
school should have advanced as
steadily as the dramatic school de-
clined from the promise of its dawn.
Born with Marlowe, it rose at once
with Shakespeare to heights inac-
cessible before and since and for
ever, to sink through bright grada-
tions of glorious decline to its final

*and beautiful sunset in Shirley:
but the lyrical record that begins
with the author of 'Euphues' and
'Endymion' grows fuller if not
brighter through a whole chain of
constellations till it culminates in
the crowning star of Herrick . . .
the greatest song-writer—as surely as Shakespeare is the greatest
dramatist—ever born of English
race."*

*The reasons for this growth and
decrease are not far to seek.
During the greater portion of the
reign of Queen Elizabeth the
newly-awaked national self-con-
sciousness had manifested itself in
so many forms that the whole field
of literature was cultivated and*

enriched. With the passing of years, however, and the aging of the Queen, the spirit of playful gallantry inseparable from a female court was gradually succeeded by a more cold and gloomy system of manners, and the poets concerned themselves more and more with subjects of an abstract or religious character.

Under King James I. (who was anxious to pass as a sacred poet and has left, amongst other works, a metrical translation of the first thirty-one Psalms) lighter poetry found little encouragement and was, in general, overweighted by the growing spirit of puritanism. The theatres alone seem to have been *the refuge of genius, and no era of English history contains so many models of dramatic excellence.*

With the accession of King Charles I. the spirit of sprightliness and courtly gallantry revived and lyric poetry resumed its place as a fine art. King Charles was, throughout his reign, a liberal patron of literature, and was repaid, in time of trouble, by a personal affection and a devoted loyalty from the poets of his court, who knew no bounds in their self-sacrifice to his cause. When soldier and courtier combined in the poet stirring and genuine verse was to be expected.

Of James Grahame, preëmi-

nently the "King's Singer," Cardinal de Retz, the friend of Condé and of Turenne, wrote—"Montrose, a Scottish nobleman, head of the house of Grahame—the only man in the world that has ever realized to me the ideas of certain heroes, whom we now discover but in the Lives of Plutarch—has sustained in his own country the cause of the King, his master, with a greatness of soul that has not found its equal in our age." Nor were there, with the exception of Wither, any of the "courtly Choir" who deserted their King when aught they could do or write might help or cheer him. The selections from their works are as *full as the limits of this volume will permit.*

Unlike most of the anthologies a fair space is here devoted to poems "divine and moral." It is a little strange that, in general, they have been so little represented, for as genuine expressions of the spirit of the age that saw the publication of the first complete and correct translation into English of the Bible, if for no other reason, they demand some recognition. Fortunately the poems of such writers as Herbert, Quarles and Crashaw are, each year, less and less neglected, and while few critics would, to-day, rank Crashaw superior to Herbert in fancy and

genius, as did Ellis in "Early
English Poets," none would agree
with the observation of the same
writer, who in commenting upon
Wotton's statement that more than
ten thousand copies of Herbert's
poems were sold during his life-
time says that it was "a circum-
stance that proves the religious
zeal much more than the good
taste of his contemporaries."
A writer in our day expressing
such an opinion might run some
risk of being counted as one

"Who says that fictions onely and false hair
    Become a verse."

Quarles has so often been de-
scribed as "quaint" that his very
modern sense of humour seems to

have been frequently overlooked. His manly vigour, his uncompromising independence, his disinterested patriotism and his exalted piety can never be entirely forgotten. There is much genuine poetry to be found in his voluminous work.

In most of the extracts modern spelling has been adopted excepting where it seemed, as with Herbert and Drayton, to be a greater loss than gain. The poems of Lovelace have so often been given in their modern form that to see them as originally printed may be a not unwelcome variation. It is rarely well to correct Kings, therefore the compositions of King

James I. and King Charles I. are left, as nearly as may be, alone.

"But," as Humphrey Moseley, stationer, writes, "I keep back the ingenuous reader by my unworthy preface. The gate is open, and thy soul invited to a garden of ravishing variety."

FitzRoy Carrington.

The
Kings' Lyrics

King James I. (1566-1625)

Ane Schort Poeme of Tyme

AS I was pansing in a morning aire,
  And could not sleip nor nawyis take me rest,
  Furth for to walk, the morning was so faire,
Athort the fields, it seemed to me the best.
The East was cleare, whereby belyve I gest
That fyrie Titan cumming was in sight,
Obscuring chaste Diana by his light.

Who by his rising in the azure skyes,
  Did dewlit helse all thanse on earth do dwell.
The balmy dew through birning drouth he dryis,
  Which made the soile to savour sweit and smell,
  By dew that on the night before downefell,
Which then was soukit up by the Delphienus heit
Up in the aire: it was so light and weit.

I

The Kings' Lyrics

Whose hie ascending in this purpour chere
    Provokit all from Morpheus to flee:
As beasts to feid, and birds to sing with beir,
    Men to their labour, bissie as the bee:
    Yet idle men devysing did I see,
How for to drive the tyme that did them irk,
By sindrie pastymes, quhile that it grew mirk.

Then woundred I to see them seik a wyle,
    So willingly the precious tyme to tine:
And how they did themselfis so farr begyle,
    To fushe of tyme, which of itself is fyne.
    Fra tyme be past to call it backward syne
Is bot in vaine: therefore men sould be warr,
To sleuth the tyme that flees fra them so farr.

For what hath man bot tyme into this life,
    Which gives him dayis his God aright to know?
Wherefore then sould we be at sic a stryfe,
    So spedelie our selfis for to withdraw
    Evin from the tyme, which is on nowayes slaw
To flie from us, suppose we fled it nought?
More wyse we were, if we the tyme had sought.

But sen that tyme is sic a precious thing,
    I wald we sould bestow it into that
Which were most pleasour to our heavenly King.

King James I

Flee ydilteth, which is the greatest lat :
Bot, sen that death to all is destinat,
Let us employ that tyme that God hath send us,
In doing well, that good men may commend us.

Sonnet

WE find by proof, that into every age
In Phœbus' art some glistering star did shine,
Who, worthy scholars to the Muses sage,
Fulfill'd their Countries with their works divine.
So Homer was a sounding trumpet fine
Amongst the Greeks, into his learned days;
So Virgil was among the Romans syne
A sprite sublim'd, a pillar of their praise !
So lofty Petrarch his renown did blaze
In tongue Italic, in a sugar'd style,
And to the circled skies his name did raise :
For he, by poems that he did compile,
Led in triumph, Love, Chasteness, Death, and Fame:
But thou triumphs o'er Petrarch's proper name !

Signed "J. Rex."

A Sonnet prefixed to Fowler's Translation of The Triumphs
of Petrarch.

3

The Kings' Lyrics

A Sonnet

Addressed by King James to his son Prince Henry

GOD gives not kings the stile of Gods in vaine,
    For on his throne his scepter do they swey:
    And as their subjects ought them to obey,
So kings should feare and serve their God againe,
If then ye would enjoy a happie reigne,
    Observe the statutes of our heavenly King:
    And from his law make all your laws to spring:
Since his lieutenant here ye should remaine,
Rewarde the just, be stedfast, true and plaine:
    Represse the proud, maintayning aye the right:
    Walke always so, as ever in His sight,
Who guardes the godly, plaguing the prophane.
    And so ye shall in princely vertues shine,
    Resembling right your mightie King divine.

Thomas Campion (—1619)

HARDEN now thy tired heart with more than
    flinty rage!
    Ne'er let her false tears henceforth thy constant
grief assuage!

4

James I. (King of England)
From the engraving by Simon van de Pass

Thomas Campion

Once true happy days thou saw'st, when she stood firm
    and kind;
Both as one then lived, and held one ear, one tongue,
    one mind:
But now those bright hours be fled and never may return:
What then remains but her untruths to mourn!

Silly trait'ress, who shall now thy careless tresses place?
Who thy pretty talk supply? whose ear thy music grace?
Who shall thy bright eyes admire, what lips triumph
    with thine?
Day by day who 'll visit thee and say "Th'art only mine"?
Such a time there was, God wot, but such shall never be.
Too oft, I fear, thou wilt remember me.

From Two Books of Airs.

LOVE me or not, love her I must or die;
    Leave me or not, follow her needs must I.
    O that her grace would my wished comforts give!
How rich in her, how happy I should live!

All my desire, all my delight should be
Her to enjoy, her to unite with me;
Envy should cease, her would I love alone:
Who loves by looks is seldom true to one.

5

The Kings' Lyrics

Could I enchant, and that it lawful were,
Her would I charm softly that none should hear:
But love enforced rarely yields firm content:
So would I love that neither should repent.

From The Fourth Book of Airs.

The Bellman's Song

MAIDS to bed and cover coal:
Let the mouse out of her hole:
Crickets in the chimney sing
Whilst the little bell doth ring:
If fast asleep, who can tell
When the clapper hits the bell?

From Melismata.

NEVER love unless you can
Bear with all the faults of man:
Men sometimes will jealous be
Though but little cause they see:
And hang the head as discontent,
And speak what straight they will repent.

Men that but one saint adore
Make a show of love to more:

6

Thomas Campion

Beauty must be scorned in none,
Though but truly served in one :
For what is courtship but disguise ?
True hearts may have dissembling eyes.

Men when their affairs require,
Must awhile themselves retire ;
Sometimes hunt and sometimes hawk,
And not ever sit and talk :
If these and such-like you can bear,
Then like, and love, and never fear !

From The Third Book of Airs.

NOW winter nights enlarge
 The number of their hours,
  And clouds their storms discharge
Upon the airy towers.
Now let the chimneys blaze,
And cups o'erflow with wine ;
Let well-tuned words amaze
With harmony divine.
Now yellow waxen lights
Shall wait on honey love,
While youthful revels, masques, and courtly sights
Sleep's leaden spells remove.

7

The Kings' Lyrics

This time doth well dispense
With lovers' long discourse:
Much speech hath some defense
Though beauty no remorse.
All do not all things well:
Some measures comely tread,
Some knotted riddles tell,
Some poems smoothly read.
The summer hath his joys
And winter his delights:
Though love and all his pleasures are but toys,
They shorten tedious nights.

From The Third Book of Airs.

Cherry Ripe

THERE is a garden in her face
    Where roses and white lilies grow:
    A heavenly paradise is that place
Wherein all pleasant fruits do flow.
  There cherries grow which none may buy,
  Till "Cherry ripe" themselves do cry.

Those cherries fairly do enclose
Of orient pearl a double row,
Which when her lovely laughter shows,

8

Robert Jones

They look like rose-buds filled with snow;
 Yet them nor peer nor prince can buy,
 Till "Cherry ripe" themselves do cry.

Her eyes, like angels, watch them still,
Her brows like bended bows do stand,
Threatening with piercing frowns to kill
All that attempt with eye or hand
 Those sacred cherries to come nigh
 Till "Cherry ripe" themselves do cry.

From The Fourth Book of Airs.

Robert Jones

AND is it night? are they thine eyes that shine?
 Are we alone, and here? and here, alone?
 May I come near, may I but touch thy shrine?
Is jealousy asleep, and is he gone?
O Gods, no more! silence my lips with thine!
Lips, kisses, joys, hap, blessing most divine!

O come, my dear! our griefs are turn'd to night,
 And night to joys: night blinds pale envy's eyes;
Silence and sleep prepare us our delight,
 O cease we then our woes, our griefs, our cries:
O vanish words! words do but passions move:
O dearest life! joy's sweet! O sweetest love!

From The Musical Dream.

The Kings' Lyrics

SOFT, Cupid, soft, there is no haste,
For all unkindness gone and past:
Since thou wilt needs forsake me so,
Let us part friends before thou go.

Still shalt thou have my heart to use, —
When otherwise I cannot chuse:
My life thou mayst command sans doubt,
Command, I say, — and go without.

And if that I do ever prove
False and unkind to gentle Love,
I'll not desire to live a day
Nor any longer — than I may.

I'll daily bless the little god, —
But not without a smarting rod.
Wilt thou still unkindly leave me?
Now I pray God, — all ill go with thee!

From The Muses' Garden of Delights.

THE sea hath many thousand sands,
The sun hath motes as many;
The sky is full of stars, and love
As full of woes as any:
Believe me, that do know the elf,
And make no trial by thyself.

Thomas Vauter

It is in truth a pretty toy
For babes to play withal;
But O the honies of our youth
Are oft our age's gall!
Self-proof in time will make thee know
He was a prophet told thee so:

A prophet that, Cassandra-like,
Tells truth without belief;
For headstrong youth will run his race,
Although his goal be grief:
Love's martyr, when his heat is past,
Proves Care's confessor at the last.

From The Muses' Garden of Delights.

Thomas Vauter

Tuwhoo, Tuwhit, Tuwhit, Tuwhoo-o-o

SWEET Suffolk owl, so trimly dight
With feathers like a lady bright,
Thou sing'st alone, sitting by night,
Te whit, te whoo!

The Kings' Lyrics

Thy note, that forth so freely rolls,
    With shrill command the mouse controls,
And sings a dirge for dying souls,
    Te whit, te whoo!

From Songs of Divers Airs and Natures.

Thomas Middleton (1570?-1627)

Simplicity

HAPPY times we live to see,
    Whose master is Simplicity:
    This is the age where blessings flow,
In joy we reap, in peace we sow;
We do good deeds without delay,
We promise and we keep our day;
We love for virtue, not for wealth,
We drink no healths but all for health;
We sing, we dance, we pipe, we play,
Our work's continual holiday;
We live in poor contented sort,
Yet neither beg nor come at court.

From The World tost at Tennis.

H. Farley

Henry Farley

A Complaint

TO see a strange outlandish fowl,
A quaint baboon, an ape, an owl,
A dancing bear, a giant's bone,
A foolish engine move alone,
A morris-dance, a puppet-play,
Mad Tom to sing a roundelay,
A woman dancing on a rope,
Bull-baiting also at the *Hope*,
A rimer's jests, a juggler's cheats,
A tumbler showing cunning feats,
Or players acting on a stage, —
There goes the bounty of our age:
But unto any pious motion
There's little coin and less devotion.
From St. Paul's Church, her Bill for the Partiment.

The Kings' Lyrics

William Drummond (1585-1649)

To a Nightingale

SWEET bird, that sing'st away the early hours
Of winters past, or coming, void of care,
  Well pleased with delights which present are,
Fair seasons, budding sprays, sweet-smelling flow'rs:
To rocks, to springs, to rills, from leavy bow'rs
Thou thy Creator's goodness dost declare,
And what dear gifts on thee he did not spare,
A stain to human sense in sin that low'rs.
What soul can be so sick, which by thy songs
(Attir'd in sweetness) sweetly is not driven
Quite to forget earth's turmoils, spites, and wrongs,
And lift a reverend eye and thought to heaven?
  Sweet, artless songster, thou my mind dost raise
  To airs of spheres, yes, and to angels' lays.

Sonnet II

I KNOW that all beneath the moon decays,
And what by mortals in this world is brought
  In Time's great periods shall return to nought:
That fairest states have fatal nights and days.

14

William Drummond of Hawthornden
After the painting by Cornelius Johnson

William Drummond

I know that all the Muses' heavenly lays,
With toil of sprite, which are so dearly bought,
As idle sounds, of few or none are sought:
That there is nothing lighter than vain praise.
I know frail beauty's like the purple flow'r,
To which one morn oft birth and death affords:
That love a jarring is of mind's accords,
Where sense and will bring under reason's power:
Know what I list, this all cannot me move,
But that, alas, I both must write and love.

Sonnet XXXVI

PHOEBUS, arise,
    And paint the sable skies
    With azure, white, and red:
Rouse Memnon's mother from her Tython's bed,
That she thy career may with roses spread,
The nightingales thy coming each where sing.
Make an eternal spring,
Give life to this dark world which lieth dead:
Spread forth thy golden hair
In larger locks than thou wast wont before,
And emperor-like decore
With diadem of pearls thy temples fair:
Chase hence the ugly night,

15

The Kings' Lyrics

Which serves but to make dear thy glorious light.
This is that happy morn,
That day, long-wished day,
Of all my life so dark,
(If cruel stars have not my ruin sworn,
And Fates my hopes betray)
Which (purely white) deserves
An everlasting diamond should it mark.
This is the morn should bring unto this grove
My love, to hear, and recompense my love.
Fair king, who all preserves,
But shew thy blushing beams,
And thou two sweeter eyes
Shalt see than those which by Peneus' streams
Did once thy heart surprise:
Nay, suns which shine as clear
As thou when two thou didst to Rome appear.
Now, Flora, deck thyself in fairest guise,
If that ye winds would hear
A voice surpassing far Amphion's lyre.
Your furious chiding stay,
Let Zephyr only breathe,
And with her tresses play,
Kissing sometimes those purple ports of death.
The winds all silent are,
And Phoebus in his chair,
Ensaffroning sea and air,

William Drummond

Makes vanish every star:
Night like a drunkard reels
Beyond the hills, to shun his flaming wheels.
The fields with flow'rs are deck'd in every hue,
The clouds with orient gold spangle their blue:
　　Here is the pleasant place,
　　And nothing wanting is, save she, alas!

Sonnet LXX

SWEET Spring, thou com'st with all thy goodly
　　train,
　　Thy head with flames, thy mantle bright with
flow'rs,
The zephyrs curl the green locks of the plain,
The clouds for joy in pearls weep down their show'rs.
Sweet Spring, thou com'st—but, ah! my pleasant hours,
And happy days, with thee come not again;
The sad memorials only of my pain
Do with thee come, which turn my sweets to sours.
Thou art the same which still thou wert before,
Delicious, lusty, amiable, fair:
But she whose breath embalm'd thy wholesome air
Is gone; nor gold, nor gems can her restore.
　　Neglected virtue, seasons go and come,
　　When thine forgot lie closed in a tomb.

17

Sonnet LXXIII

MY lute, be as thou wert when thou didst grow
With thy green mother in some shady grove,
When immelodious winds but made thee move
And birds their ramage did on thee bestow.
Since that dear voice which did thy sounds approve,
Which wont in such harmonious strains to flow,
Is reft from earth to tune those spheres above,
What art thou but a harbinger of woe?
Thy pleasing notes be pleasing notes no more,
But orphans' wailings to the fainting ear,
Each stroke a sigh, each sound draws forth a tear,
For which be silent as in woods before:
    Or if that any hand to touch thee deign,
    Like widow'd turtle still her loss complain.

Of a Bee

O DO not kill that bee
That thus hath wounded thee!
Sweet, it was no despite,
But hue did him deceive:
For when thy lips did close,
He deemed them a rose.

18

King Charles I

What wouldst thou further crave?
He wanting wit, and blinded with delight,
Would fain have kiss'd, but mad with joy did bite.

King Charles I. (1600-1649)

Majesty in Misery

GREAT Monarch of the world, from whose power
springs
The potency and power of kings,
Record the royal woe my suffering sings;

And teach my tongue, that ever did confine
Its faculties in truth's seraphick line,
To track the treasons of thy foes and mine.

Nature and law, by thy divine decree,
(The only root of righteous royaltie)
With this dim diadem invested me:

With it, the sacred scepter, purple robe,
The holy unction, and the royal globe:
Yet am I levell'd with the life of Job.

The fiercest furies, that do daily tread
Upon my grief, my grey discrowned head,
Are those that owe my bounty for their bread.

19

The Kings' Lyrics

They raise a war, and christen it THE CAUSE,
While sacriligeous hands have best applause,
Plunder and murder are the kingdom's laws:

Tyranny bears the title of taxation,
Revenge and robbery are reformation,
Oppression gains the name of sequestration.

My loyal subjects, who in this bad season
Attend me (by the law of God and reason),
They dare impeach, and punish for high treason.

Next at the clergy do their furies frown,
Pious episcopacy must go down,
They will destroy the crosier and the crown.

Churchmen are chain'd and schismaticks are freed,
Mechanicks preach, and holy fathers bleed,
The crown is crucified with the creed.

The Church of England doth all factions foster,
The pulpit is userpt by each impostor,
Extempore excludes the *Paternoster.*

The Presbyter and Independent seed
Spring with broad blades. To make religion bleed
Herod and Pontius Pilate are agreed.

King Charles I

The corner stone's misplac'd by every pavier:
With such a bloody method and behaviour
Their ancestors did crucifie our Saviour.

My royal consort, from whose fruitful womb
So many princes legally have come,
Is forc'd in pilgrimage to seek a tomb.

Great Britain's heir is forced into France,
Whilst on his father's head his foes advance:
Poor child! he weeps out his inheritance.

With my own power my majesty they wound,
In the king's name the king himself's uncrown'd:
So doth the dust destroy the diamond.

With propositions daily they enchant
My people's ears, such as do reason daunt,
And the Almighty will not let me grant.

They promise to erect my royal stem,
To make me great, t' advance my diadem,
If I will first fall down, and worship them!

But for refusal they devour my thrones,
Distress my children, and destroy my bones:
I fear they 'll force me to make bread of stones.

The Kings' Lyrics

My life they prize at such a slender rate,
That in my absence they draw bills of hate,
To prove the king a traytor to the state.

Felons obtain more privilege than I,
They are allow'd to answer ere they die:
'Tis death for me to ask the reason why.

But, sacred Saviour, with thy words I woo
Thee to forgive, and not be bitter to
Such, as thou know'st do not know what they do.

For, since they from their Lord are so disjointed,
As to contemn those edicts he appointed,
How can they prize the power of his anointed?

Augment my patience, nullifie my hate,
Preserve my issue, and inspire my mate,
Yet, though we perish, BLESS THIS CHURCH AND
    STATE.

Written while prisoner in Carisbrook Castle.

On a *Quiet Conscience*

CLOSE thine eyes, and sleep secure;
Thy soul is safe, thy body sure.
He that guards thee, he that keeps,

George Sandys

Never slumbers, never sleeps.
A quiet conscience in the breast
Has only peace, has only rest.
The wisest and the mirth of kings
Are out of tune unless she sings:
Then close thine eyes in peace and sleep secure,
No sleep so sweet as thine, no rest so sure.

George Sandys (1577-1643)

To King Charles I.

THE Muse who from your influence took her birth,
First wander'd through the many-peopled earth;
Next sung the change of things, disclos'd th' un-
known,
Then to a nobler shape transform'd her own:
Fetch'd from Engaddi spice, from Jewry balm,
And bound her brows with Idumæan palm:
Now, old, hath her last voyage made, and brought
To royal harbour this her sacred fraught:
Who to her King bequeathes the wealth of kings:
And dying, her own epicedium sings.

23

The Kings' Lyrics

To the Queen

CHASTE Nymph, you who extracted are
From that swift Thunderbolt of war; *
Whose innocence and meekness prove
An eagle may beget a dove;
In this clear mirror you may find
The image of your own fair mind;
With each attractive excellence,
Which feasts the more refinèd sense;
The crownèd muse from heav'n inspir'd
With such rich beauties hath attir'd
The Sacred Spouse: for what below
The sun could more perfection show?

Dedication of A Paraphrase upon the Songs of Solomon.

THOU brought'st me home in safety, that this earth
Might bury me, which fed me from my birth:
Blest with a healthful age, a quiet mind,
Content with little, to this work design'd;
Which I at length have finish'd by Thy aid,
And now my vows have at Thy altar paid.

From Deo Opt. Max. *at the conclusion of the* Paraphrases.

* Henrietta Maria, daughter of Henry IV. of France.

24

James Graham (*Marquis of Montrose*)
From the engraving by Houbraken
after the painting by William Dobson

J. Grahame

ames Grahame, Marquis of Montrose (1612-1650)

My Dear and Only Love

MY dear and only love, I pray
　　That little world, — of Thee, —
　Be governed by no other way
Than purest monarchy.
For if confusion have a part,
　Which virtuous souls abhor,
I 'll call a Synod in mine heart,
　And never love thee more.

As Alexander I will reign,
　And I will reign alone :
My thoughts did evermore disdain
　A rival on my throne :
He either fears his fate too much,
　Or his deserts are small,
That dares not put it to the touch,
　To gain or lose it all.

The Kings' Lyrics

But I will reign and govern still,
    And always give the law,
And have each subject at my will,
    And have all stand in awe.
But 'gainst my batteries if I find
    Thou kick or vex me sore,
As that thou set me up a blind,
    I 'll never love thee more.

And in the empire of thine heart,
    Where I should solely be,
If others do pretend a part,
    Or dare to vie with me:
Or if *committees* thou erect,
    And go on such a score,
I 'll laugh and sing at thy neglect,
    And never love thee more.

But if thou wilt prove faithful then,
    And constant of thy word,
I'll make thee famous by my pen,
    And glorious by my sword:
I 'll serve thee in such noble ways
    Was never heard before,
I 'll crown and deck thee all with bays,
    And love thee more and more.

26

George Wither
From the engraving by John Payne

George Wither

On the Execution of Charles I.

GREAT, good, and just, could I but rate
My grief with thy too rigid fate,
I'd weep the world in such a strain
As it should deluge once again;
But since thy loud-tongued blood demands supplies
More from Briareus' hands than Argus' eyes,
I'll sing thy obsequies with trumpet sounds,
And write thy epitaph in blood and wounds.

George Wither (1588-1667)

Sonnet

SHALL I, wasting in despair,
Die because a woman's fair?
Or make pale my cheeks with care
'Cause another's rosy are?
Be she fairer than the day,
Or the flowery meads in May:
If she be not so to me,
What care I how fair she be?

The Kings' Lyrics

Shall my foolish heart be pin'd,
'Cause I see a woman kind?
Or a well-disposed nature
Joined with a lovely feature?
Be she meeker, kinder, than
Turtle-dove or pelican:
   If she be not so to me,
    What care I how kind she be?

Shall a woman's virtues move
Me to perish for her love?
Or her merit's value known,
Make me quite forget mine own?
Be she with that goodness blest
Which may gain her name of *best*;
   If she be not such to me,
    What care I how good she be?

'Cause her fortune seems too high,
Shall I play the fool and die?
Those that bear a noble mind
Where they want of riches find,
Think what with them they would do,
That without them dare to woo:
   And unless that mind I see,
    What care I though great she be?

George Wither

Great, or good, or kind, or fair,
I will ne'er the more despair:
If she love me, this believe,
I will die e'er she shall grieve:
If she slight me when I woo,
I can scorn and let her go;
    For if she be not for me,
    What care I for whom she be?

Sonnet upon a Stolen Kiſs

NOW gentle sleep hath closed up those eyes
    Which, waking, kept my boldest thoughts in awe;
    And free access unto that sweet lip lies,
From whence I long the rosy breath to draw.
Methinks no wrong it were, if I should steal
From those two melting rubies, one poor kiss:
None sees the theft that would the theft reveal,
Nor rob I her of ought what she can miss:
Nay should I twenty kisses take away,
There would be little sign I would do so;
Why then should I this robbery delay?
Oh! she may wake, and therewith angry grow!
Well, if she do, I'll back restore that one,
And twenty hundred thousand more for loan.

The Kings' Lyrics

AMARYLLIS I did woo,
And I courted Phillis too;
Daphne for her love I chose;
Chloris for that damask rose
In her cheek I held as dear;
Yea, a thousand lik'd, well-near;
And, in love with all together,
Feared the enjoying either;
'Cause to be of one possest,
Barr'd the hope of all the rest.

LORDLY gallants, tell me this:
Though my safe content you weigh not,
In your greatness what one bliss
Have you gain'd that I enjoy not?
You have honours, you have wealth;
I have peace, and I have health;
All the day I merry make,
And at night no care I take.

Bound to none my fortunes be:
This or that man's fall I fear not;
Him I love that loveth me;
For the rest a pin I care not.

30

George Wither

You are sad when others chafe,
And grow merry as they laugh!
I, that hate it, and am free,
Laugh and weep as pleaseth me.

HENCE, away, thou Siren, leave me!
    Pish! unclasp these wanton arms!
    Sugar'd words can ne'er deceive me,
Though thou prove a thousand charms.
    Fie, fie, forbear!
    No common snare
Can ever my affection chain:
    Thy painted baits,
    And poor deceits,
Are all bestow'd on me in vain.

I'm no slave to such as you be,
    Nor shall that soft snowy breast,
Rolling eye, and lip of ruby,
    Ever rob me of my rest.
    Go, go display
    Thy beauty's ray
To some more-soon-enamour'd swain:

The Kings' Lyrics

Those forced wiles
Of sighs and smiles
Are all bestow'd on me in vain.

I have elsewhere vow'd a duty;
  Turn away thy tempting eye:
Shew not me thy painted beauty;
  These impostures I defy.
    My spirit loaths
    Where gaudy clothes
And feigned oaths may love obtain:
    I love her so
    Whose looks swear no
That all thy labour will be vain.

Can he prize the tainted posies
  Which on other's breast are worn,
That may pluck the virgin roses
  From the never-touched thorn?
    I can go rest
    On her sweet breast
That is the pride of Cynthia's train:
    Then stay thy tongue,
    Thy mermaid song
Is all bestow'd on me in vain.

George Wither

He's a fool that basely dallies
  Where each peasant mates with him.
Shall I haunt the thronged vallies,
  Whilst there's noble hills to climb?
    No, no;—though clowns
    Are scar'd with frowns,
I know the best can but disdain:
    And those I'll prove,
    So will thy love
Be all bestow'd on me in vain.

*   *   *   *   *

I do scorn to vow a duty
  Where each lustful lad may woo
Give me her whose sun-like beauty
  Buzzards dare not soar unto.
    She, she it is
    Affords that bliss
For which I would refuse no pain:
    But such as you,
    Fond fools, adieu!
You seek to captive me in vain.

*   *   *   *   *

The Kings' Lyrics

Leave me then, thou Siren, leave me!
　Seek no more to work my harms:
Crafty wiles cannot deceive me;
　I am proof against your charms.
　　You labour may
　　To lead astray
The heart that constant shall remain;
　　And I the while
　　Will sit and smile
To see you spend your time in vain.

A Dirge

FAREWELL,
Sweet groves, to you!
You hills that highest dwell,
And all you humble vales adieu!
You wanton brooks, and solitary rocks;
My dear companions all, and you my tender flocks!
Farewell, my pipe! and all those pleasing songs, whose moving strains
Delighted once the fairest nymphs that dance upon the plains.
You discontents, whose deep and over-deadly smart
Have without pity broke the truest heart,
Sighs, tears, and every sad annoy,
That erst did with me dwell,
And others joy
Farewell!

34

William Browne (1590-1650?)

Song of the Sirens

STEER hither, steer your wingèd pines,
    All-beaten mariners!
  Here lie Love's undiscovered mines,
    A prey to passengers;
Perfumes far sweeter than the best
Which make the Phœnix' urn and nest.
    Fear not your ships,
Nor any to oppose you save our lips;
    But come on shore
Where no joy dies till love hath gotten more.

For swelling waves our panting breasts,
    Where never storms arise,
Exchange, and be awhile our guests:
    For stars gaze on our eyes.
The compass love shall hourly sing,
And as he goes about the ring,
    We will not miss
To tell each point he nameth with a kiss.
Chorus:
    Then come on shore,
Where no joy dies till love hath gotten more.

From The Inner Temple Masque.

The Kings' Lyrics

Venus and Adonis

VENUS by Adonis' side
   Crying kiss'd and kissing cried:
   Wrung her hands and tore her hair
For Adonis dying there.

Stay! quoth she: O stay and live!
Nature surely does not give
To the earth her sweetest flowers
To be seen but some few hours.

On his face, still as he bled,
For each drop a tear she shed,
Which she kiss'd or wiped away,—
Else had drown'd him where he lay.

Fair Proserpina, quoth she,
Shall not have thee yet from me:
Nor thy soul to fly begin
While my lips can keep it in.

Here she closed again. And some
Say—Apollo would have come
To have cured his wounded limb—
But that she had smother'd him.

Robert Herrick

From the engraving by William Marshall

Robert Herrick (1591-1674)

Delight in Diſorder

A SWEET disorder in the dress
Kindles in clothes a wantonness:
A lawn about the shoulders thrown
Into a fine distraction:
An erring lace which here and there
Enthrals the crimson stomacher:
A cuff neglectful, and thereby
Ribbons to flow confusedly:
A winning wave, deserving note,
In the tempestuous petticoat :
A careless shoe-string, in whose tie
I see a wild civility:
Do more bewitch me than when art
Is too precise in every part.

The Bag of the Bee

A BOUT the sweet bag of a bee
Two cupids fell at odds,
And whose the pretty prize should be
They vow'd to ask the gods.

37

The Kings' Lyrics

Which Venus hearing, thither came,
    And for their boldness stripp'd them,
And, taking thence from each his flame,
    With rods of myrtle whipp'd them.

Which done, to still their wanton cries,
    When quiet grown she'd seen them,
She kiss'd, and wip'd their dove-like eyes,
    And gave the bag between them.

The Captiv'd Bee, or the Little Filcher

AS Julia once a-slumbering lay
    It chanced a bee did fly that way,
    After a dew or dew-like shower,
To tipple freely in a flower.
For some rich flower he took the lip
Of Julia, and began to sip;
But when he felt he sucked from thence
Honey, and in the quintessence,
He drank so much he scarce could stir,
So Julia took the pilferer.

Robert Herrick

And thus surprised, as filchers use,
He thus began himself t' excuse:
Sweet lady-flower, I never brought
Hither the least one thieving thought;
But, taking those rare lips of yours
For some fresh, fragrant, luscious flowers.
I thought I might there take a taste,
Where so much syrup ran at waste.
Besides, know this: I never sting
The flower that gives me nourishing;
But with a kiss, or thanks, do pay
For honey that I bear away.
This said, he laid his little scrip
Of honey 'fore her ladyship:
And told her, as some tears did fall,
That that he took, and that was all.
At which she smiled, and bade him go
And take his bag: but thus much know:
When next he came a-pilfering so,
He should from her full lips derive
Honey enough to fill his hive.

The Kings' Lyrics

To the Virgins, to Make Much of Time

GATHER ye rosebuds while ye may,
  Old time is still a-flying:
And this same flower that smiles to-day
To-morrow will be dying.

The glorious lamp of heaven, the sun,
  The higher he's a-getting,
The sooner will his race be run,
  And nearer he's to setting.

That age is best which is the first,
  When youth and blood are warmer:
But being spent, the worse, and worst
  Times still succeed the former.

Then be not coy, but use your time,
  And while ye may go marry:
For having lost but once your prime
  You may for ever tarry.

Robert Herrick

Upon Cupid

AS lately I a garland bound,
'Mongst roses I there Cupid found;
I took him, put him in my cup,
And drunk with wine, I drank him up.
Hence then it is that my poor breast
Could never since find any rest.

To Meadows

YE have been fresh and green,
    Ye have been fill'd with flowers,
    And ye the walks have been
Where maids have spent their hours.

You have beheld how they
    With wicker arks did come
To kiss and bear away
    The richer cowslips home.

You've heard them sweetly sing,
    And seen them in a round:
Each virgin like a spring,
    With honeysuckles crown'd.

41

The Kings' Lyrics

But now we see none here
 Whose silvery feet did tread,
And with dishevell'd hair
 Adorn'd this smoother mead.

Like unthrifts, having spent
 Your stock and needy grown,
You're left here to lament
 Your poor estates, alone.

Devotion Makes the Deity

WHO forms a godhead out of gold or stone
Makes not a god, but he that prays to one.

To Daffodils

FAIR daffodils, we weep to see
 You haste away so soon;
As yet the early-rising sun
Has not attain'd his noon.
 Stay, stay,
Until the hasting day
 Has run

Robert Herrick

But to the evensong;
And, having prayed together, we
Will go with you along.

We have short time to stay, as you,
We have as short a spring;
As quick a growth to meet decay,
As you, or anything.
We die,
As your hours do, and dry
Away,
Like to the summer's rain;
Or as the pearls of morning's dew,
Ne'er to be found again.

To Daifies, not to Shut fo Soon

SHUT not so soon; the dull-ey'd night
Has not as yet begun
To make a seizure on the light,
Or to seal up the sun.

No marigolds yet closèd are,
No shadows great appear;
Nor doth the early shepherd's star
Shine like a spangle here.

The Kings' Lyrics

Stay but till my Julia close
  Her life-begetting eye,
And let the whole world then dispose
  Itself to live or die.

To Bloſſoms

FAIR pledges of a fruitful tree,
    Why do ye fall so fast?
    Your date is not so past
But you may stay yet here a while,
    To blush and gently smile:
      And go at last.

What! were ye born to be
    An hour or half's delight,
    And so to bid good-night?
'Twas pity Nature brought ye forth
    Merely to show your worth,
      And lose you quite.

But you are lovely leaves, where we
    May read how soon things have
    Their end, though ne'er so brave:
And after they have shown their pride
    Like you a while, they glide
      Into the grave.

44

George Herbert
After the engraving by R. White

G. Herbert

George Herbert (1593-1633)

Eafter

I HAD preparèd many a flowre
To straw Thy way and vi&ctesla;orie:
   But Thou wast up before myne houre,
Bringinge Thy sweets along with Thee.

The sunn arising in the East,
Though hee bring light and th' other sents,
Can not make up so braue a feast,
As Thy discouerie presents.

Yet though my flours be lost, they say
A hart can never come too late:
Teach it to sing Thy praise this day,
And then this day my life shall date.

Sinne

LORD, with what care hast Thou begirt us round!
   Parents first season us: then schoolmasters
   Deliver us to laws; they send us, bound
To rules of reason, holy messengers,

The Kings' Lyrics

Pulpits and Sundayes, sorrow dogging sinne,
  Afflictions sorted, anguish of all sizes,
  Fine nets and stratagems to catch us in,
Bibles laid open, millions of surprises:

Blessings beforehand, tyes of gratefulnesse,
  The sound of glorie ringing in our eares,
  Without, our shame; within, our consciences;
Angels and grace, eternall hopes and fears.

  Yet all these fences and their whole aray
  One cunning bosome-sinne blows quite away.

Jordan

WHO says that fictions onely and false hair
      Become a verse? Is there in truth no beautie?
      Is all good structure in a winding-stair?
May no lines passe, except they do their dutie
  Not to a true, but painted chair?

Is it not verse, except enchanted groves
And sudden arbours shadow coarse-spunne lines?
Must purling streams refresh a lover's loves?
Must all be vail'd while he that reades divines,
  Catching the sense at two removes?

46

George Herbert

Shepherds are honest people, let them sing:
Riddle who list, for me, and pull for prime,
I envie no man's nightingale or spring:
Nor let them punish me with loss of rhyme,
   Who plainly say, My God, my King.

Church Muſick

SWEETEST of sweets, I thank you: when dis-
    pleasure
   Did through my bodie wound my minde,
You took me thence, and in your house of pleasure
   A daintie lodging me assign'd.

Now I in you without a bodie move,
   Rising and falling with your wings:
We both together sweetly live and love,
   Yet say sometimes, "God help poore kings!"

Comfort, I'le die; for if you poste from me,
   Sure I shall do so, and much more:
But if I travell in your companie,
   You know the way to heaven's doore.

The Kings' Lyrics

The Quidditie

MY God, a verse is not a crown,
No point of honour, or gay suit,
No hawk, or banquet, or renown,
Nor a good sword, nor yet a lute.

It cannot vault, or dance, or play,
It never was in France or Spain,
Nor can it entertain the day
With a great stable or demain.

It is no office, art, or news,
Nor the Exchange, or busie hall:
But it is that which, while I use,
I am with Thee: and "MOST TAKE ALL."

Avarice

MONEY, thou bane of blisse and source of wo,
Whence com'st thou, that thou art so fresh
and fine?
I know thy parentage is base and low,—
Man found thee poore and dirtie in a mine.

George Herbert

Surely thou didst so little contribute
    To this great kingdome which thou now hast got,
    That he was fain, when thou wert destitute,
To digge thee out of thy dark cave and grot.

Then forcing thee, by fire he made thee bright:
    Nay, thou hast got the face of man; for we
    Have with our stamp and seal transferred our right;
Thou art the man, and man but drosse to thee.

Man calleth thee his wealth, who made thee rich;
And while he digs out thee, falls in the ditch.

The World

L OVE built a stately house, where Fortune came;
    And spinning phansies, she was heard to say
    That her fine cobwebs did support the frame,
Whereas they were supported by the same;
But Wisdome quickly swept them all away.

Then Pleasure came, who, liking not the fashion,
Began to make balcónes, terraces,
Till she had weaken'd all by alteration;
But rev'rend laws, and many a proclamation,
Reformèd all at length with menaces.

The Kings' Lyrics

Then enter'd Sinne, and with that sycamore
Whose leaves first sheltred man from drought and dew,
Working and winding slily evermore,
The inward walls and sommers* cleft and tore; *Main
But Grace shor'd these, and cut that as it grew. beams.

Then Sinne combin'd with Death in a firm band
To rase the building to the very floore:
Which they effected, none could them withstand;
But Love took Grace and Glorie by the hand,
And built a braver palace then before.

The Quip

THE merrie World did on a day
With his train-bands and mates agree
To meet together where I lay,
And all in sport to geere at me.

First Beautie crept into a rose,
Which when I pluckt not, "Sir," said she,
"Tell me, I pray, whose hands are those?"
But Thou shalt answer, Lord, for me.

George Herbert

Then Money came, and chinking still,
"What tune is this, poore man?" said he;
"I heard in Musick you had skill:"
But Thou shalt answer, Lord, for me.

Then came brave Glorie puffing by
In silks that whistled, who but he!
He scarce allowed me half an eie:
But Thou shalt answer, Lord, for me.

Then came quick Wit and Conversation
And he would needs a comfort be,
And, to be short, make an oration:
But Thou shalt answer, Lord, for me.

Yet when the houre of Thy designe
To answer these fine things shall come,
Speak not at large, say, I am Thine,
And then they have their answer home.

Love

LOVE bade me welcome; yet my soul drew back,
    Guilty of dust and sin.
But quick-ey'd Love, observing me grow slack

The Kings' Lyrics

From my first entrance in,
Drew nearer to me, sweetly questioning
   If I lack'd any thing.

"A guest," I answered, "worthy to be here:"
   Love said, "You shall be he."
"I, the unkind, ungrateful? Ah, my dear,
   I cannot look on Thee."
Love took my hand, and smiling did reply,
   "Who made the eyes but I?"

"Truth, Lord: but I have marr'd them: let my shame
   Go where it doth deserve."
"And know you not," says Love, "Who bore the
   blame?"
   "My dear, then I will serve."
"You must sit down," says Love, "and taste My meat."
   So I did sit and eat.

Thomas Carew (1598-1638)

Ingrateful Beauty Threatened

KNOW, *Celia*, since thou art so proud,
   'Twas I that gave thee thy renown.
   Thou had'st in the forgotten crowd

Thomas Carew
After the painting by Sir Anthony Van Dyck

Thomas Carew

Of common Beauties lived unknown,
Had not my verse extoll'd thy name,
And with it ympt* the wings of Fame.

That killing power is none of thine:
    I gave it to thy voice and eyes;
Thy sweets, thy graces, all are mine;
    Thou art my Star, shin'st in my skies:
Then dart not from thy borrow'd sphere
Lightning on him that fix'd thee there.

Tempt me with such affrights no more,
    Lest what I made I uncreate:
Let fools thy mystic forms adore,
    I know thee in thy Mortal state.
Wise poets that wrapt Truth in tales,
Knew her themselves through all her veils.

Disdain Returned

HE that loves a rosy cheek,
    Or a coral lip admires,
        Or, from star-like eyes, doth seek
Fuel to maintain his fires;
As old Time makes these decay,
So his flames must waste away.

* *This phrase is borrowed from Falconry. To ymp is to add
a new piece to a broken feather in tail or wing.*

The Kings' Lyrics

But a smooth and steadfast mind,
  Gentle thoughts and calm desires,
Hearts with equal love combined,
  Kindle never-dying fires.
Where these are not, I despise
Lovely cheeks, or lips, or eyes.

No tears, *Celia*, now shall win
  My resolved heart to return;
I have search'd thy soul within,
  And find nought but pride and scorn.
I have learn'd thy arts, and now
Can disdain as much as thou.
  Some Power in my revenge convey
  That Love to her I cast away.

On Celia Singing to her Lute, in Arundel Garden

HARK, how my *Celia*, with the choice
  Music of her hand and voice,
    Stills the loud wind, and makes the wild
Enraged boar and panther mild.
Mark how those statues like men move,

Thomas Carew

While men with wonder statues prove.
  The stiff rock bends to worship her:
  The Idol turns idolater.

Now, see how all the new inspired
Images with love are fired!
Hark how the tender marble groans,
And all the late transformed stones
Court the fair Nymph, with many a tear,
Which she—more stony than they were—
Beholds with unrelenting mind;
When they, amazed to see combined
  Such matchless beauty with disdain,
  Are all turn'd into stone again.

Ask Me no more where Jove Bestows

ASK me no more, where *Jove* bestows,
  When *June* is past, the fading rose?
   For in your Beauty's orient deep
These flowers, as in their causes, sleep.

  Ask me no more, whither do stray
The golden atoms of the day?
For in pure love heaven did prepare
Those powders to enrich your hair.

The Kings' Lyrics

Ask me no more, whither doth haste
The Nightingale, when *May* is past?
For in your sweet dividing throat
She winters and keeps warm her note.

Ask me no more, where those stars 'light,
That downwards fall in dead of night?
For in your eyes they sit, and there
Fixed become, as in their sphere.

Ask me no more, if east or west
The Phœnix builds her spicy nest?
For unto you at last she flies,
And in your fragrant bosom dies.

The Hue and Cry

IN Love's name you are charged hereby
To make a speedy "Hue and Cry"
After a face, which t'other day,
Stole my wand'ring heart away.
To direct you, these, in brief,
Are ready marks to know the Thief.

Her hair a net of beams would prove
Strong enough to captive *Jove*,
In his Eagle's shape; her brow

Thomas Carew

Is a comely field of snow;
Her eye so rich, so pure a grey,
Every beam creates a day:
 And, if she but sleep (not when
 The sun sets), 'tis Night again.

 In her cheeks are to be seen
Of flowers both the King and Queen,
Thither by the Graces led,
And freshly laid in nuptial bed;
On whose lips, like-Nymphs do wait,
Who deplore their virgin state:
 Oft they blush, and blush for this,
 That they one another kiss.

 But observe, besides the rest,
You shall know this Felon best
By her tongue; for if your ear
Once a heavenly music hear,
Such as neither gods nor men—
But from that voice—shall hear again,
That, that is she. O! straight surprise,
And bring her unto Love's Assize.
If you let her go, she may
Ante-date the Latter Day,
 Fate and Philosophy controul,
 And leave the world without a soul.

The Kings' Lyrics

The Tooth-ache Cured by a Kiſs

FATE'S now grown merciful to men,
  Turning disease to bliss:
  For had not kind rheum vext me, then,
I might not *Celia* kiss.
Physicians, you are now my scorn,
  For I have found a way
To cure diseases — when forlorn
  By your dull art — which may
Patch up a body for a time:
  But can restore to health
No more than 'chymists can sublime
  True Gold, the *Indies'* wealth.
That Angel sure, that used to move
  The Pool* men so admired,   *Bethesda*.
Hath to her lip, the seat of Love,
  As to his heaven, retired.

Thomas Carew

On his Mistress Going to Sea

FAREWELL, fair Saint! may not the sea and wind
Swell like the hearts and eyes you leave behind:
But calm and gentle, as the looks you bear,
Smile in your face, and whisper in your ear.

Let no bold billow offer to arise,
That it may nearer gaze upon your eyes:
Lest wind and wave, enamour'd of your form,
Should throng and crowd themselves into a storm.

But if it be your fate, vast Seas! to love,
Of my becalmed breast learn how to move;
Move then, but in a gentle Lover's pace:
No wrinkle, nor no furrow, in your face.

And you, fierce Winds, see that you tell your tale
In such a breath as may but fill her Sail:
So, whilst you court her, each your several way,
You may her safely to her Port convey,
And loose her, by the noblest way of Wooing:
Whilst both contribute to your own undoing.

The Kings' Lyrics

Eternity's Song

BE fixed, you rapid Orbs, that bear
 The changing seasons of the year
 On your swift wings, and see the old
Decrepit Sphere grown dark and cold:
Nor did *Jove* quench her fires: these bright
Flames have eclipsed her sullen light:
This Royal Pair, for whom Fate will
Make Motion cease, and Time stand still:
Since Good is here so perfect, as no Worth
Is left for After-Ages to bring forth.

From Cœlum Britannicum, A Masque.

Sir *Richard Fanſhawe* (1607-1666)

Of Beauty

LET us use it while we may
 Snatch those joys that haste away!
 Earth her winter coat may cast,
And renew her beauty past:
But, our winter come, in vain
We solicit Spring again;
And when our furrows snow shall cover
Love may return, but never lover.

60

Sir John Suckling
From the engraving by George Vertue
after the painting by Sir Anthony Van Dyck

Sir J. Suckling

Sir John Suckling (1609-1641)

Ballad upon a Wedding

(Written upon the occasion of the marriage of
Roger Boyle, 1st Earl of Orrery with Lady Mar-
garet Howard, daughter of Theophilus, Earl of
Suffolk.)

I TELL thee, Dick, where I have been,
  Where I the rarest things have seen:
    O, things without compare!
Such sights again cannot be found
In any place on English ground,
    Be it at wake or fair.

At Charing Cross, hard by the way,
Where we (thou know'st) do sell our hay,
    There is a house with stairs:
And there did I see coming down
Such folks as are not in our town,
    Forty, at least, in pairs.

Amongst the rest, one pest'lent fine
(His beard no bigger though than Thine)
    Walked on before the rest:

The Kings' Lyrics

Our landlord looks like nothing to him:
The King (God bless him) 'twould undo him,
　　Should he go still so drest.

At Course-a-Park, without all doubt,
He should have first been taken out
　　By all the maids i' th' town:
Though lusty Roger there had been,
Or little George upon the Green,
　　Or Vincent of the Crown.

But, wot you what? the youth was going
To make an end of all his wooing:
　　The parson for him stay'd:
Yet by his leave (for all his haste)
He did not so much wish all past
　　(Perchance) as did the maid.

The maid (and thereby hangs a tale,
For such a maid not Whitsun-ale
　　Could ever yet produce)
No grape, that's kindly ripe, could be
So round, so plump, so soft as she,
　　Nor half so full of juice.

Her finger was so small, the ring
Would not stay on, which they did bring,
　　It was too wide a peck:

Sir John Suckling

And to say truth (for out it must)
It looked like the great collar (just)
   About our young colt's neck.

Her feet beneath her petticoat,
Like little mice, stole in and out,
   As if they fear'd the light:
But O she dances such a way!
No sun upon an Easter day
   Is half so fine a sight.

He would have kissed her once or twice
But she would not, she was so nice,
   She would not do 't in sight,
And then she looked as who should say:
I will do what I list to-day,
   And you shall do 't at night.

Her cheeks so rare a white was on,
No daisy makes comparison
   (Who sees them is undone),
For streaks of red were mingled there,
Such as are on a Cath'rine pear
   (The side that's next the sun).

Her lips were red, and one was thin,
Compared to that was next her chin
   (Some bee had stung it newly):

The Kings' Lyrics

But, Dick, her eyes so guard her face;
I durst no more upon them gaze
   Than on the sun in July.

Her mouth so small, when she does speak,
Thou'dst swear her teeth her words did break,
   That they might passage get;
But she so handled still the matter,
They came as good as ours, or better,
   And are not spent a whit.

  ✳   ✳   ✳   ✳   ✳   ✳   ✳

Passion o'me, how I run on!
There's that that would be thought upon
   (I trow) besides the bride;
The business of the kitchen's great,
For it is fit that man should eat;
   Nor was it there denied:

Just in the nick the cook knocked thrice,
And all the waiters in a trice
   His summons did obey;
Each serving-man, with dish in hand,
Marched boldly up, like our trained band,
   Presented, and away.

64

Sir John Suckling

When all the meat was on the table,
What man of knife or teeth was able
    To stay to be intreated?
And this the very reason was,
Before the parson could say grace,
    The company was seated.

Now hats fly off, and youths carouse:
Healths first go round, and then the house,
    The bride's came thick and thick:
And when 'twas nam'd another's health,
Perhaps he made it hers by stealth:
    And who could help it, Dick?

On the sudden up they rise and dance:
Then sit again and sigh, and glance:
    Then dance again and kiss:
Thus several ways the time did pass,
Whilst ev'ry woman wished her place,
    And every man wished his.

By this time all were stol'n aside
To counsel and undress the bride:
    But that he must not know:

But yet 'twas thought he guess'd her mind,
And did not mean to stay behind
Above an hour or so.

✳ ✳ ✳ ✳ ✳ ✳ ✳ ✳

Note. *"This ballad may safely be pronounced his Opus Magnum; indeed, for grace and simplicity it stands un- rivalled in the whole compass of ancient and modern poetry."* — William Wordsworth.

A Supplement of an Imperfect copy of Verses of Mr. William Shakespeare's

ONE of her hands one of her cheeks lay under,
Cozening the pillow of a lawful kiss,
Which therefore swelled, and seemed to part asunder,
As angry to be robbed of such a bliss!
The one looked pale and for revenge did long,
While t'other blushed, 'cause it had done the wrong.

Out of the bed the other fair hand was
On a green satin quilt, whose perfect white
Looked like a daisy in a field of grass," *
And showed like unmelt snow unto the sight;
There lay this pretty perdue, safe to keep
The rest o' th' body that lay fast asleep.

* *Thus far Shakespeare.*

Sir John Suckling

Her eyes (and therefore it was night), close laid,
Strove to imprison beauty till the morn:
But yet the doors were of such fine stuff made,
That it broke through, and showed itself in scorn,
Throwing a kind of light about the place;
Which turned to smiles still, as 't came near her face.

Her beams, which some dull men called hair, divided,
Part with her cheeks, part with her lips did sport.
But these, as rude, her breath put by still; some
Wiselier downward sought, but falling short,
Curled back in rings, and seemed to turn again
To bite the part unkindly held them in.

DOST see how unregarded now
 That piece of beauty passes?
There was a time when I did vow
 To that alone:
 But mark the fate of faces;
The red and white works now no more on me,
Than if it could not charm, or I not see.

And yet the face continues good,
 And still I have desires,
And still the self-same flesh and blood,
 As apt to melt,

The Kings' Lyrics

And suffer from those fires:
O, some kind power unriddle where it lies:
Whether my heart be faulty, or her eyes?

She every day her man doth kill,
    And I as often die:
Neither her power then nor my will
    Can questioned be;
  What is the mystery?
Sure, beauty's empires, like to greater states,
Have certain periods set, and hidden fates.

The Metamorphosis

THE little boy, to show his might and power,
    Turn'd Io to a cow, Narcissus to a flower;
    Transformed Apollo to a homely swain,
And Jove himself into a golden rain.
These shapes were tolerable, but by the Mass
He's metamorphosed me into an Ass!

Sir John Suckling

The Falſe One

HAST thou seen the down in the air
   When wanton blasts have tossed it?
     Or the ship on the sea,
When ruder winds have crossed it?
Hast thou marked the crocodile's weeping,
   Or the fox's sleeping?
Or hast viewed the peacock in his pride,
   Or the dove by his bride,
When he courts for his lechery?
O, so fickle, O, so vain, O, so false, so false is she!

From **The Sad One.**

A Soldier

I AM a man of war and might,
And know thus much, that I can fight,
Whether I am i' th' wrong or right,
      Devoutly.
No woman under heaven I fear,
New oaths I can exactly swear,
And forty healths my brain will bear
      Most stoutly.

69

The Kings' Lyrics

I cannot speak, but I can do
As much as any of our crew;
And if you doubt it, some of you
                    May prove me.
I dare be bold thus much to say,
If that my bullets do but play,
You would be hurt so night and day,
                    Yet love me.

Orſames' Song

WHY so pale and wan, fond lover?
        Prithee, why so pale?
        Will, when looking well can't move her,
Looking ill prevail?
Prithee, why so pale?

Why so mute and dumb, young sinner?
    Prithee, why so mute?
Will, when speaking well can't win her,
    Saying nothing do't?
    Prithee, why so mute?

Sir John Suckling

Quit, quit, for shame, this will not move :
  This cannot take her.
If of herself she will not love,
  Nothing can make her :
  The devil take her !

The Conſtant Lover

OUT upon it! I have loved
  Three whole days together ;
  And am like to love three more,
If it prove fine weather.

Time shall moult away his wings,
  Ere he shall discover
In the whole wide world again
  Such a constant lover.

But the spite on 't is, no praise
  Is due at all to me :
Love with me had made no stays,
  Had it any been but she.

Had it any been but she,
  And that very face,
There had been at least, ere this,
  A dozen in her place !

71

The Kings' Lyrics

I PRITHEE send me back my heart,
Since I cannot have thine :
For if from yours you will not part,
Why then shouldst thou have mine?

Yet now I think on 't, let it lie,
To find it, were in vain,
For th' hast a thief in either eye
Would steal it back again.

Why should two hearts in one breast lie,
And yet not lodge together?
O love! where is thy sympathy,
If thus our breasts you sever?

But love is such a mystery,
I cannot find it out:
For when I think I 'm best resolv'd,
I then am most in doubt.

Then farewell care, and farewell woe,
I will no longer pine :
For I 'll believe I have her heart,
As much as she has mine.

Sir John Suckling

Love and Debt

THERE'S one request I make to Him,
Who sits the clouds above:
That I were fairly out of debt,
As I am out of love.

Then for to dance, to drink, to sing
I should be very willing:
I should not owe one lass a kiss,
Nor any rogue a shilling.

'Tis only being in love or debt,
That robs us of our rest,
And he that is quite out of both,
Of all the world is blest.

He sees the golden age, wherein
All things were free and common:
He eats, he drinks, he takes his rest—
And fears nor man nor woman.

William Cartwright (1611-1643)

Lesbia on her Sparrow

TELL me not of joy! there's none,
 Now my little sparrow's gone:
  He, just as you,
  Would sigh and woo,
He would chirp and flatter me:
  He would hang the wing a while,
  Till at length he saw me smile,
Lord! how sullen he would be!

He would catch a crumb, and then
Sporting let it go again:
  He from my lip
  Would moisture sip,
He would from my trencher feed:
  Then would hop, and then would run,
  And cry *Phillip* when he'd done:
Oh! whose heart can choose but bleed?

Oh! how eager would he fight,
And ne'er hurt though he did bite.
  No morn did pass,

William Cartwright

But on my glass
He would sit, and mark, and do
    What I did; now ruffle all
    His feathers o'er, now let them fall,
And then straightway sleek them too.

Whence will Cupid get his darts
Feather'd now, to pierce our hearts?
    A wound he may,
    Not love, convey,
Now this faithful bird is gone.
    Oh! let mournful turtles join
    With loving redbreasts, and combine
To sing dirges o'er his stone.

To Chloe

Who wished herself young enough for me.

CHLOE, why wish you that your years
    Would backwards run, till they meet mine?
    That perfect likeness, which endears
Things unto things, might us combine.
Our ages so in date agree,
That twins do differ more than we.

The Kings' Lyrics

There are two births, the one when light
   First strikes the new awakened sense;
The other when two souls unite:
   And we must count our life from thence:
When you lov'd me, and I lov'd you,
Then both of us were born anew.

Love then to us did new souls give,
   And in those souls did plant new pow'rs:
Since when another life we live,
   The breath is his, not ours:
Love makes those young whom age doth chill,
And whom he finds young keeps young still.

Love, like that angel that shall call
   Our bodies from the silent grave,
Unto one age doth raise us all;
   None too much, none too little have:
Nay, that the difference may be none,
He makes two not alike, but one.

And now since you and I are such,
   Tell me what's yours, and what is mine?
Our eyes, our ears, our taste, smell, touch,
   Do, like our souls, in one combine;
So, by this, I as well may be
Too old for you, as you for me.

FRANCIS QUARLES.

Francis Quarles
From the engraving by I. Wright

F. Quarles

Francis Quarles (1592-1664)

Song of Anarchus

KNOW then, my brethren, heaven is clear,
   And all the clouds are gone;
   The righteous now shall flourish, and
Good days are coming on:
Come then, my brethren, and be glad,
And eke rejoice with me;
Lawn sleeves and rochets shall go down,
And hey! then up go we!

We 'll break the windows which the whore
Of Babylon hath painted,
And when the popish saints are down,
Then Barrow shall be sainted.
There 's neither cross nor crucifix
Shall stand for men to see;
Rome's trash and trumperies shall go down,
And hey! then up go we!

   *   *   *   *   *   *   *

We 'll down with all the *'Varsities,*
Where learning is profess'd,
Because they practice and maintain

The Kings' Lyrics

The language of the beast.
We'll drive the doctors out of doors,
And arts, whate'er they be:
We'll cry both arts and learning down,
And hey! then up go we!

*　　*　　*　　*　　*　　*　　*

If once that Anti-christian crew
Be crush'd and overthrown,
We'll teach the nobles how to crouch,
And keep the gentry down.
Good manners have an ill report,
And turn to pride we see:
We'll therefore cry good manners down,
And hey! then up go we!

The name of lord shall be abhorr'd,
For every man's a brother:
No reason why, in church, or state,
One man should rule another.
But when the change of government
Shall set our fingers free,
We'll make the wanton sisters stoop,
And hey! then up go we!

Our cobblers shall translate their *souls*
From caves obscure and shady:
We'll make Tom T—— as good as my lord,

Francis Quarles

And Joan as good as my lady.
We 'll crush and fling the marriage ring
Into the Roman *see;*
We 'll ask no bands, but e'en clap hands,
And hey! then up go we!

From Shepherd's Oracles.

WHAT, Cupid, are thy shafts already made?
And seeking honey to set up thy trade,
True emblem of thy sweets! thy bees do bring
Honey in their mouths, but in their tails a sting.

Epigram No. 3, Book 1.

Non omne quod hic micat aurum eft

FALSE world, thou ly'st; thou canst not lend
The least delight:
Thy favours cannot gain a friend,
They are so slight:
Thy morning pleasures make an end
To please at night:
Poor are the wants that thou supply'st;
And yet thou vaunt'st, and yet thou vy'st
With Heaven; fond earth, thou boast'st, false world,
thou ly'st.

79

The Kings' Lyrics

Thy babbling tongue tells golden tales
    Of endless treasure:
Thy bounty offers easy sales
    Of lasting pleasure;
Thou ask'st the conscience what she ails,
    And swear'st to ease her:
There's none can want where thou supply'st,
There's none can give where thou deny'st,
Alas! fond world, thou boast'st; false world, thou ly'st

What well advised ear regards
    What Earth can say?
Thy words are gold, but thy rewards
    Are painted clay:
Thy cunning can but pack the cards,
    Thou canst not play:
Thy game at weakest still thou vy'st;
If seen, and then revy'd, deny'st:
Thou art not what thou seem'st; false world, thou ly'st

Thy tinsel bosom seems a mint
    Of new-coin'd treasure;
A paradise that has no stint,
    No change, no measure;
A painted cask, but nothing in't
    Nor wealth nor pleasure:

Francis Quarles

Vain earth! that falsely thus comply'st
With man; vain man, that thou rely'st
On earth; vain man, thou doat'st; vain earth, thou ly'st.

What mean dull souls, in this high measure
   To haberdash
In earth's base wares, whose greatest treasure
   Is dross and trash?
The height of whose enchanting pleasure
   Is but a flash?
Are these the goods that thou supply'st
Us mortals with? Are these the high'st?
Can these bring cordial peace? False world, thou ly'st.

                From Emblems, Divine and Moral.

MY heart! but wherefore do I call thee so?
   I have renounc'd my int'rest long ago:
     When thou wert false and fleshly, I was thine;
Mine wert thou never, till thou wert not mine.

                Epigram No. 15, Book 2.

The Kings' Lyrics

LOOK not, my watch, being once repair'd, to stand
Expecting motion from thy Maker's hand.
He's wound thee up, and cleans'd thy clogs with
blood:
If now thy wheels stand still, thou art not good.

Epigram No. 8, Book 4.

Sic decipit orbis

BELIEVE her not, her glass diffuses
False portraitures: thou canst espy
No true reflection: she abuses
Her misinform'd beholder's eye;
Her crystal's falsely steel'd; it scatters
Deceitful beams; believe her not, she flatters.

This flaring mirror represents
No right proportion, view or feature:
Her very looks are compliments;
They make thee fairer, goodlier, greater:
The skilful gloss of her reflection
But paints the context of thy coarse complexion.

Francis Quarles

Were thy dimension but a stride,
Nay, wert thou statur'd but a span,
Such as the long-bill'd troops defied,
A very fragment of a man!
She'll make thee Mimas, which you will,
The Jove-slain tyrant, or th' Ionic hill.

Had surfeits, or th' ungracious star,
Conspir'd to make one commonplace
Of all deformities that are
Within the volume of thy face,
She'd lend thee favour should outmove
The Troy-bane Helen, or the Queen of Love.

Were thy consum'd estate as poor
As Laz'rus or afflicted Job's:
She'll change thy wants to seeming store,
And turn thy rags to purple robes;
She'll make thy hide-bound flank appear
As plump as theirs that feast it all the year.

Look off, let not thy optics be
Abus'd: thou seest not what thou should'st:
Thyself's the object thou should'st see,
But 'tis the shadow thou behold'st:
And shadows thrive the more in stature,
The nearer we approach the light of nature.

The Kings' Lyrics

Where Heav'n's bright beams look more direct,
The shadow shrinks as they grow stronger.
But when they glance their fair aspect,
The bold-fac'd shade grows larger, longer:
And when their lamp begins to fall,
Th' increasing shadows lengthen most of all.

The soul that seeks the noon of grace,
Shrinks in, but swells if grace retreat.
As Heav'n lifts up, or veils his face,
Our self-esteems grow less or great.
The least is greatest, and who shall
Appear the greatest, are the least of all.

From Emblems, Divine and Moral.

WHAT need that house be daub'd with flesh and
   blood?
   Hung round with silks and gold? repair'd with
   food?
Cost idly spent! that cost doth but prolong
Thy thraldom. Fool, thou mak'st thy jail too strong.

Epigram No. 8, Book 5.

W. Habington

William Habington (1605-1654)

*To Caſtara**

Softly singing to herself

SING forth, sweet Cherubin (for we have choice
Of reasons in thy beauty, and thy voice,
To name thee so, and scarce appear prophane)
Sing forth, that while the orbs celestial straine
To echo thy sweet note, our human ears
May then receive the music of the spheres,
But yet take heed, lest if the swans of Thames,
That add harmonious pleasure to the streams,
O' th' sudden hear thy well-divided breath,
Should listen, and in silence welcome death:
And ravisht nightingales, striving too high
To reach thee, in the emulation die.
    And thus there will be left no bird to sing
    Farewell to th' waters, welcome to the spring.

** Lucia Habington, his wife, daughter of William Lord
Powis.*

The Kings' Lyrics

Defcription of Caftara

LIKE the violet, which alone
   Prospers in some happy shade:
   My Castara lives unknown,
To no looser eye betray'd,
  For she 's to her self untrue,
  Who delights i' th' public view.

Such is her beauty, as no arts
Have enricht with borrowed grace,
Her high birth no pride imparts,
For she blushes in her place.
  Folly boasts a glorious blood,
  She is noblest being good.

Cautious, she knew never yet
What a wanton courtship meant:
Not speaks loud to boast her wit,
In her silence eloquent.
  Of herself survey she takes,
  But 'tween men no difference makes.

She obeys with speedy will
Her grave parents' wise commands.
And so innocent, that ill,

William Habington

She nor acts, nor understands.
  Women's feet run still astray,
  If once to ill they know the way.

She sails by that rock, the Court,
Where oft honour splits her mast:
And retir'dness thinks the port,
Where her fame may anchor cast.
  Vertue safely cannot sit,
  Where vice is enthron'd for wit.

She holds that day's pleasure best,
Where sin waits not on delight;
Without mask, or ball, or feast,
Sweetly spends a winter's night.
  O'er that darkness whence is thrust
  Prayer, and sleep oft governs lust.

She her throne makes reason climb,
While wild passions captive lie;
And each article of time,
Her pure thoughts to Heaven fly:
  All her vows religious be,
  And her love she vows to me.

The Kings' Lyrics

To the Spring

Upon the uncertainty of Castara's abode

FAIR mistress of the Earth, with garlands crown'd,
   Rise, by a lover's charm: from the parcht ground,
   And show thy flowery wealth: that she, where ere
Her stars shall guide her, meet thy beauties there.
Should she to the cold northern climates go,
Force the affrighted lillies there to grow,
Thy roses in those gelid fields t' appear;
She absent, I have all their winter here.
Or if to th' torrid zone her way she bend,
Her the cool breathing of Favonius lend.
Thither command the birds to bring their quires;
That zone is temp'rate, I have all his fires.
   Attend her, courteous Spring, though we should here
   Lose by it all the treasures of the year.

T. Nabbes

Thomas Nabbes (1612?———)

a Mistress of whose Affection He was Doubtful

WHAT though with figures I should raise
Above all height my mistress' praise;
Calling her cheek a blushing rose,
The fairest June did e'er disclose;
Her forehead, lilies; and her eyes,
The luminaries of the skies;
That on her lips ambrosia grows,
And from her kisses nectar flows?—
Too great hyperboles! unless
She loves me, she is none of these.
But, if her heart and her desires
Do answer mine with equal fires,
These attributes are then too poor,—
She is all these, and ten times more.

The Kings' Lyrics

Richard Crashaw (1612-1648)

The Weeper

HAIL sister Springs,
Parents of silver-footed rills!
Ever bubbling things!
Thawing crystal! Snowy hills!
Still spending, never spent; I mean
Thy fair eyes, sweet Magdalene.

Heavens thy fair eyes be;
Heavens of ever-falling stars;
'Tis seed-time still with thee,
And stars thou sow'st, whose harvest dares
Promise the earth to countershine
Whatever makes Heaven's forehead fine.

(And 29 other verses.
From Steps to the Temple

A Song

LORD, when the sense of Thy sweet grace
Sends up my soul to seek Thy face,
Thy blessed eyes breed such desire,

Richard Crashaw

I die in Love's delicious fire.
O Love! I am Thy sacrifice,
Be still triumphant, blessed eyes;
Still shine on me, fair suns, that I
Still may behold though still I die.

Though still I die, I live again,
Still longing so to be still slain;
So gainful is such loss of breath,
I die even in desire of death.
Still live in me this loving strife
Of living death and dying life:
For while thou sweetly slayest me,
Dead to myself, I live in Thee.

From Carmen Deo Nostro.

The Widow's Mites

TWO mites, two drops, yet all her house and land,
  Fall from a steady heart, though trembling hand:
  The other's wanton wealth foams high, and brave:
The other cast away, she only gave.

From Divine Epigrams.

The Kings' Lyrics

THOUGH now 'tis neither May nor June,
   And nightingales are out of tune,
   Yet in these leaves, fair One, there lies
(Sworn servant to your sweetest eyes)
A nightingale, who, may she spread
In your white bosom her chaste bed,
Spite of all the maiden snow
Those pure untrodden paths can show,
You straight shall see her wake and rise,
Taking fresh life from your fair eyes,
And with claspt wings proclaim a spring,
Where Love and she shall sit and sing;
For lodged so near your sweetest throat
What nightingale can lose her note?
Nor let her kindred birds complain
Because she breaks the year's old reign:
For let them know she's none of those
Hedge-quiristers whose music owes
Only such strains as serve to keep
Sad shades, and sing dull night asleep.
No, she's a priestess of that grove,
The holy chapel of chaste love,
Your virgin bosom. Then whate'er
Poor laws divide the public year,
Whose revolutions wait upon
The wild turns of the wanton sun,

In memoriam fratris desideratissimi delini Fran: Lovelace.

Richard Lovelace
From the engraving by Hollar
after the drawing by Colonel Francis Lovelace

Richard Lovelace

Be you the Lady of Love's year,
Where your eyes shine his suns appear,
There all the year is Love's long Spring,
  There all the year
Love's nightingales shall sit and sing.

Richard Lovelace (1618-1658)

---

o Lucafta. Going to the Warres

TELL me not, (sweet,) I am unkinde,
    That from the nunnerie
    Of thy chaste breast and quiet minde
To warre and armes I flie.

True: a new Mistress now I chase,
  The first foe in the field,
And with a stronger faith embrace
A sword, a horse, a shield.

Yet this inconstancy is such,
  As you too shall adore;
I could not love thee, dear, so much,
  Lov'd I not Honour more.

93

The Kings' Lyrics

Lucaſta Weeping

LUCASTA wept, and still the bright
  Inamour'd god of day,
  With his soft handkercher of light,
Kist the wet pearles away.

But when her teares his heate or'ecame
  In cloudes he quensht his beames,
And griev'd, wept out his eye of flame,
  So drownèd her sad streames.

At this she smiled, when straight the sun
  Cleer'd by her kinde desires;
And by her eyes' reflexion
  Fast kindl'd there his fires.

Upon the Curtaine of Lucaſta's Picture

OH, stay that covetous hand; first turn all eye,
  All depth and minde; then mystically spye
  Her soul's faire picture, her faire soul's, in al
So truely copied from th' originall,
That you will sweare her body by this law
Is but its shadow, as this, its; — now draw.

94

Richard Lovelace

Ellinda's Glove

THOU snowy farme with thy five tenements!
    Tell thy white mistris here was one,
    That call'd to pay his dayly rents;
But she a-gathering flow'rs and hearts is gone,
And thou left voyd to rude possession.

But grieve not, pretty Ermin cabinet,
    Thy alabaster lady will come home;
    If not, what tenant can there fit
The slender turnings of thy narrow roome,
But must ejected be by his owne dombe?

Then give me leave to leave my rent with thee:
    Five kisses, one unto a place:
    For though the lute's too high for me,
Yet servants, knowing minikin nor base,
Are still allow'd to fiddle with the case.

The Graſſehopper

To my noble friend, Mr. Charles Cotton

OH thou, that swing'st upon the waving eare
    Of some well-fillèd oaten beard,
    Drunk ev'ry night with a delicious teare
Dropt thee from Heav'n, where now th' art reard.

The Kings' Lyrics

The joyes of earth and ayre are thine intire,
  That with thy feet and wings doth hop and flye;
And when thy poppy workes, thou dost retire
  To thy carv'd acorn-bed to lye.

Up with the day, the Sun thou welcomst then,
  Sportst in the guilt plats of his beames,
And all these merry dayes mak'st merry men,
  Thy selfe, and melancholy streames.

But ah, the sickle! golden eares are cropt;
  Ceres and *Bacchus* bid good night;
Sharpe frosty fingers all your flowrs have topt,
  And what sithes spar'd, winds shave off quite.

Poore verdant foole! and now green ice, thy joys
  Large and as lasting as thy peirch of grasse,
Bid us lay in 'gainst winter raine, and poize
  Their flouds with an o'erflowing glasse.

Thou best of men and friends! we will create
  A genuine summer in each other's breast;
And spite of this cold Time and frozen Fate,
  Thaw us a warm seate to our rest.

Our sacred harthes shall burne eternally
  As vestal flames; the North-wind, he
Shall strike his frost-stretch'd winges, dissolve and fl[:]
  This Ætna in epitome.

96

Richard Lovelace

Dropping December shall come weeping in,
  Bewayle th' usurping of his raigne;
But when in show'rs of old Greeke* we beginne,
  Shall crie, he hath his crowne againe!   *Greek
                                           Wine

Night as cleare Hesper shall our tapers whip
  From the light casements, where we play,
And the dark hagge from her black mantle strip,
  And sticke there everlasting day.

Thus richer then untempted kings are we,
  That asking nothing, nothing need:
Though lord of all what seas imbrace, yet he
  That wants himselfe, is poore indeed.

The Vintage to the Dungeon

SING out, pent soules, sing cheerefully!
  Care shackles you in liberty:
    Mirth frees you in captivity.
  Would you double fetters adde?
  Else why so sadde?

Chorus:
  Besides your pinion'd armes youl finde
  Griefe too can manakell the minde.

97

The Kings' Lyrics

Live then, pris'ners, uncontroll'd:
Drink o' th' strong, the rich, the old,
Till wine too hath your wits in hold:
  Then if still your jollitie
  And throats are free —

Chorus:
  Tryumph in your bondes and paines,
  And dance to the music of your chaines.

To Althea

From Prison

WHEN love with unconfinèd wings
    Hovers within my gates:
  And my divine *Althea* brings
To whisper at the grates;
When I lye tangled in her haire,
  And fettered to her eye,
The birds, that wanton in the aire,
  Know no such liberty.

When flowing cups run swiftly round
  With no allaying *Thames,*
Our carelesse heads with roses bound,
  Our hearts with loyal flames:

Richard Lovelace

When thirsty griefe in wine we steepe,
   When healths and draughts go free,
Fishes, that tipple in the deepe,
   Know no such libertie.

When (like committed linnets) I
   With shriller throat shall sing
The sweetnes, mercy, majesty,
   And glories of my King.
When I shall voyce aloud, how good
   He is, how great should be,
Inlargèd winds, that curle the flood,
   Know no such liberty.

Stone walls doe not a prison make,
   Nor iron bars a cage;
Mindes innocent and quiet take
   That for an hermitage:
If I have freedome in my love,
   And in my soule am free,
Angels alone that sore above
   Enjoy such liberty.

Richard Brome (16.. -1652)

Beggars' Song

COME! Come away! the Spring,
By every bird that can but sing
Or chirp a note, doth now invite
Us forth to taste of his delight,
In field, in grove, on hill, in dale;
But above all the nightingale,
Who in her sweetness strives t' outdo
The loudness of the hoarse cuckoo.
"Cuckoo," cries he; "Jug, jug, jug," sings she;
From bush to bush, from tree to tree:
Why in one place then tarry we?

Come away! Why do we stay?
We have no debts or rent to pay;
No bargains or accounts to make,
Nor land nor lease, to let or take:
Or if we had, should that remore* us
When all the world's our own before us,
And where we pass and make resort,

* *Remore*—hinder: from *Remora*, the name of a fish supposed
to stick to ships and retard their progress.

James Shirley
After the original picture in the Bodleian Gallery

James Shirley

It is our kingdom and our court.
"Cuckoo," cries he: "Jug, jug, jug," sings she:
From bush to bush, from tree to tree:
Why in one place then tarry we?

From A Jovial Crew, or the Merry Beggars.

James Shirley (1594-1666)

Peace Reſtored

YOU virgins, that did late despair
    To keep your wealth from cruel men,
  Tie up in silk your careless hair:
Soft peace is come again.

Now lovers' eyes may gently shoot
  A flame that will not kill;
The drum was angry, but the lute
  Shall whisper what you will.

Sing Io, Io! for his sake
  That hath restored your drooping heads:
With choice of sweetest flowers make
  A garden where he treads:

The Kings' Lyrics

Whilst we whole groves of laurel bring,
    A petty triumph for his brow,
Who is the master of our spring
    And all the bloom we owe.

From The Imposture.

Death's Subtle Ways

VICTORIOUS men of earth, no more
        Proclaim how wide your empires are;
    Though you bind in every shore
And your triumphs reach as far
        As night or day,
    Yet you, proud monarchs, must obey
And mingle with forgotten ashes when
Death calls ye to the crowd of common men.

Devouring Famine, Plague, and War,
    Each able to undo mankind,
Death's servile emissaries are;
    Nor to these alone confined,
        He hath at will
    More quaint and subtle ways to kill;
A smile or kiss, as he will use the art,
Shall have the cunning skill to break a heart.

From Cupid and Death; A Masque.

102

James Shirley

No Armour Againſt Fate

THE glories of our blood and state
    Are shadows, not substantial things;
    There is no armour against Fate:
Death lays his icy hand on kings:
      Sceptre and crown
      Must tumble down,
And in the dust be equal made
With the poor crooked scythe and spade.

Some men with swords may reap the field,
    And plant fresh laurels where they kill:
But their strong nerves at last must yield:
    They tame but one another still:
      Early or late,
      They stoop to fate,
And must give up their murmuring breath,
When they, pale captives, creep to death.

The garlands wither on your brow,
    Then boast no more your mighty deeds;
Upon Death's purple altar now,
    See where the victor-victim bleeds:
      Your heads must come
      To the cold tomb:
Only the actions of the just
Smell sweet and blossom in their dust.

        From The Contention of Ajax and Ulysses.

John Milton (1608-1674)

On May Morning

NOW the bright Morning Star, day's harbinger,
Comes dancing from the east, and leads with her
The flowery May, who from her green lap throws
The yellow cowslip, and the pale primrose.
Hail, bounteous May, that dost inspire
Mirth, and youth, and warm desire!
Woods and groves are of thy dressing,
Hill and dale doth boast thy blessing:
Thus we salute thee with our early song,
And welcome thee, and wish thee long!

O'er the Smooth Enamelled Green

O'ER the smooth enamelled green,
Where no print of step hath been,
Follow me, as I sing
And touch the warbled string:
Under the shady roof
Of branching elm star-proof

John Milton
From the engraving by George Vertue

John Milton

Follow me.
I will bring you where she sits,
Clad in splendour, as befits
     Her deity.
Such a rural queen
All Arcadia hath not seen.

From Arcades.

---

mphs and Shepherds, Dance no More

NYMPHS and shepherds, dance no more
     By sandy Ladon's lilied banks:
     On old Lycæus or Cyllene hoar,
Trip no more in twilight ranks:
Though Erymanth your loss deplore,
     A better soil shall give ye thanks.
From the stony Mænalus
Bring your flocks and live with us:
Here ye shall have better grace,
To serve the Lady of this place.
Though Syrinx your Pan's mistress were,
Yet Syrinx well might wait on her.
Such a rural queen
All Arcadia hath not seen.

From Arcades.

The Kings' Lyrics

BY the rushy-fringèd bank,
  Where grows the willow and the osier dank,
  My sliding chariot stays,
Thick set with agate, and the azure sheen
Of turquoise blue, and emerald green,
That in the channel strays;
Whilst from off the waters fleet
Thus I set my printless feet
O'er the cowslip's velvet head,
That bends not as I tread;
Gentle swain, at thy request
I am here.

From Comus

On the Nightingale

O NIGHTINGALE, that on yon bloomy spray
  Warblest at eve, when all the woods are still,
  Thou with fresh hope the lover's heart dost fill
While the jolly hours lead on propitious May.
Thy liquid notes that close the eye of day,
First heard before the shallow cuckoo's bill,
Portend success in love. Oh, if Jove's will

John Milton

Have link'd that amourous power to thy soft lay,
Now timely sing, ere the rude bird of hate
Foretell my hopeless doom in some grove nigh:
As thou from year to year hast sung too late
For my relief, yet hadst no reason why:
Whether the Muse, or Love, call thee his mate,
Both them I serve, and of their train am I.

Lux Haeres nulla tibi Warwici villa, tenebris,
Ante tuas Cunas, obsita) Prima fuit.
Arma, Viros, Veneres, Patriam modulamine dixti;
Te Patriae resonant Arma, Viri, Veneres.

Michael Drayton
After the engraving by William Hole

HE BALLAD OF AGINCOURT

BY

Michael Drayton

M. Drayton

Michael Drayton (1563-1631)

To my Frinds the Camber-Britans and theyr Harp

FAYRE stood the winde for France,
 When we our sailes aduance,
 Nor now to proue our chance
Longer not tarry,
But put vnto the mayne:
At Kaux, the mouth of Seine,
With all his warlike trayne
 Landed King Harry.

And taking many a forte,
Furnish'd in warlike sorte,
Comming toward Agincourte
 (In happy houre)
Skermishing day by day
With those oppose his way,
Whereas the Cenrall laye
 With all his powre.

III

The Kings' Lyrics

Which in his height of pride,
As Henry to deride,
His ransome to prouide
   Unto him sending:
Which he neglects the while,
As from a nation vyle,
Yet with an angry smile
   Their fall portending.

And turning to his men,
Quoth famous Henry then,
Though they be one to ten,
   Be not amazed:
Yet haue we well begun:
Battailes so brauely wonne
Euermore to the sonne
   By fame are raysed.

And for my selfe, (quoth hee)
This my full rest shall bee,
England nere mourne for me,
   Nor more esteeme me:
Victor I will remaine,
Or on this earth be slaine:
Neuer shall she sustaine
   Losse to redeeme me.

Michael Drayton

Poiters and Cressy tell,
When moste their pride did swell,
Under our swords they fell:
   Ne lesse our skill is,
Then when our grandsyre greate,
Claiming the regall seate,
In many a warlike feate
   Lop'd the French lillies.

The Duke of York soe dread
The eager vaward led;
With the maine Henry sped
   Amongst his hench men.
Excester had the rear,
A brauer man not there.
And now preparing were
   For the false Frenchmen

And ready to be gone.
Armour on armour shone,
Drum unto drum did grone,
   To hear was woonder;
That with the cries they make
The very earth did shake:
Trumpet to trumpet spake,
   Thunder to thunder.

The Kings' Lyrics

Well it thine age became,
O, noble Erpingham !
That didst the signall frame
   Unto the forces :
When from a medow by,
Like a storme, sodainely
The English archery
   Stuck the French horses.

The Spanish ughe so strong,
Arrowes a cloth-yard long,
That like to serpents stoong,
   Piercing the wether :
None from his death now starts,
But playing manly parts,
And like true English harts
   Stuck close together.

When down theyr bowes they threw,
And foorth theyr bilbowes drewe,
And on the French they flew,
   No man was tardy.
Arms from the shoulders sent,
Scalps to the teeth were rent :
Downe the French pesants went
   These were men hardye.

Michael Drayton

When now that noble King,
His broad sword brandishing,
Into the hoast did fling,
   As to or'whelme it;
Who many a deep wound lent,
His armes with blood besprent,
And many a cruell dent
   Brused his helmett.

Glo'ster that Duke so good,
Next to the royall blood,
For famous England stood
   With his braue brother:
Clarence in steele most bright,
That yet a maiden knighte,
Yet in this furious fighte
   Scarce such an other.

Warwick in blood did wade,
Oxford the foes inuade,
And cruel slaughter made
   Still as they ran up:
Suffolk his axe did ply,
Beaumont and Willoughby
Bare them right doughtyly,
   Ferrers and Fanhope.

The Kings' Lyrics

On happy Cryspin day
Fought was this noble fray,
Which fame did not delay
   To England to carry.
O! when shall Englishmen
With such acts fill a pen,
Or England breed agen
   Such a King Harry?

F I N I S

INDEX TO AUTHORS

With first Lines of their Poems

117

The Kings' Lyrics

Index to Authors

The Kings' Lyrics

James I., King (1566-1625)

Jones, Robert

Lovelace, Richard (1618-1658)

Middleton, Thomas (1570?-1627)

Index to Authors

The Kings' Lyrics

THE TABLE

or, Index to first Lines

The Kings' Lyrics

F

Index to First Lines

I

K

L

The Kings' Lyrics

Index to First Lines

The Kings' Lyrics

*Printed for R. H. Ruſſell by
D. B. Updike, The Merrymount
Preſs, at the Sign of the Maypole,
104 Cheſtnut Street, Boſton*